Fish Don't Play Ball

Emma McCann

Albury Children's

Bob was just dozing off to sleep
when Sam burst in with something
LARGE and INTERESTING.

"Look Bob!" said Sam,
very excited.

"Dad bought me a
goldfish! Isn't it great?
It's called Fish."

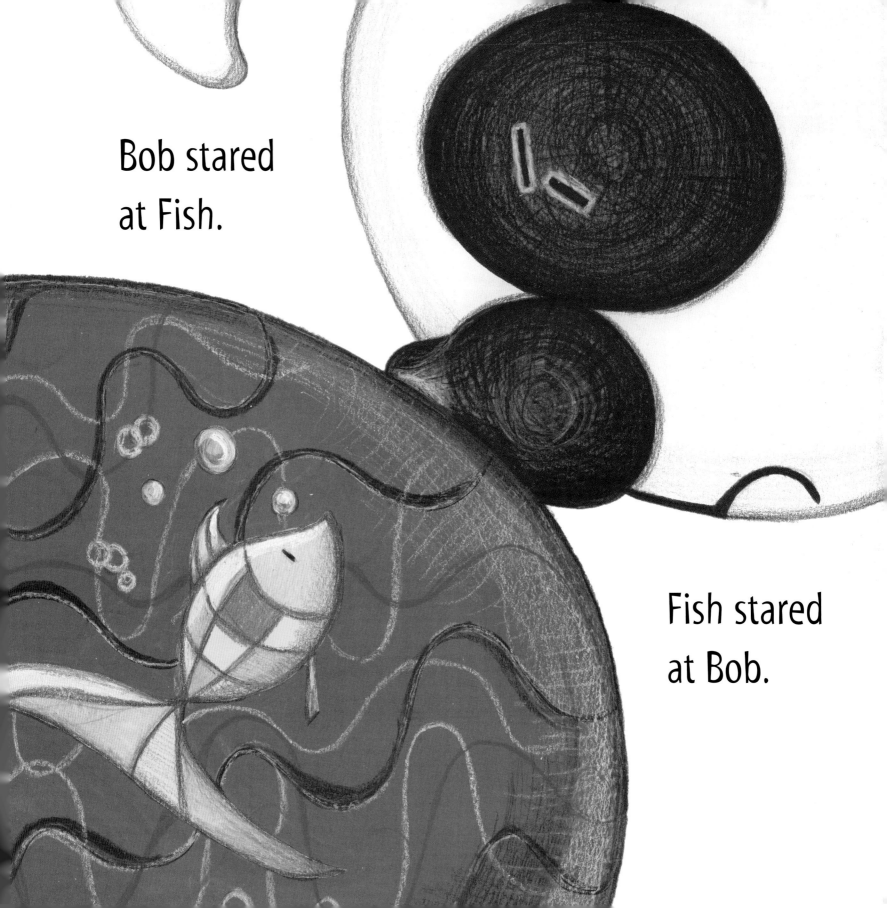

Bob stared
at Fish.

Fish stared
at Bob.

It didn't look great to Bob.
It looked a bit…

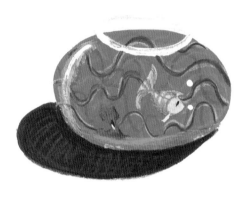

…well, not much fun, actually.

Bob decided he'd come back later when Fish
was doing something
more interesting…

... like juggling,
or something.

Bob watched
Fish from under
the table.

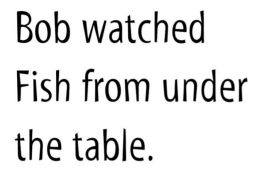

He watched Fish
from behind the
curtains.

He even watched
Fish from the
garden (and it
was raining
too!).

Obviously, Fish just
didn't know what to do.

(Bob decided to help...)

"Perhaps Fish would like to play
ball with me," thought Bob.
Bob tried very hard to play ball
with Fish...

...but Fish just wasn't
very good at it.

The ball just floated on top of the water.
Fish wouldn't throw it back.

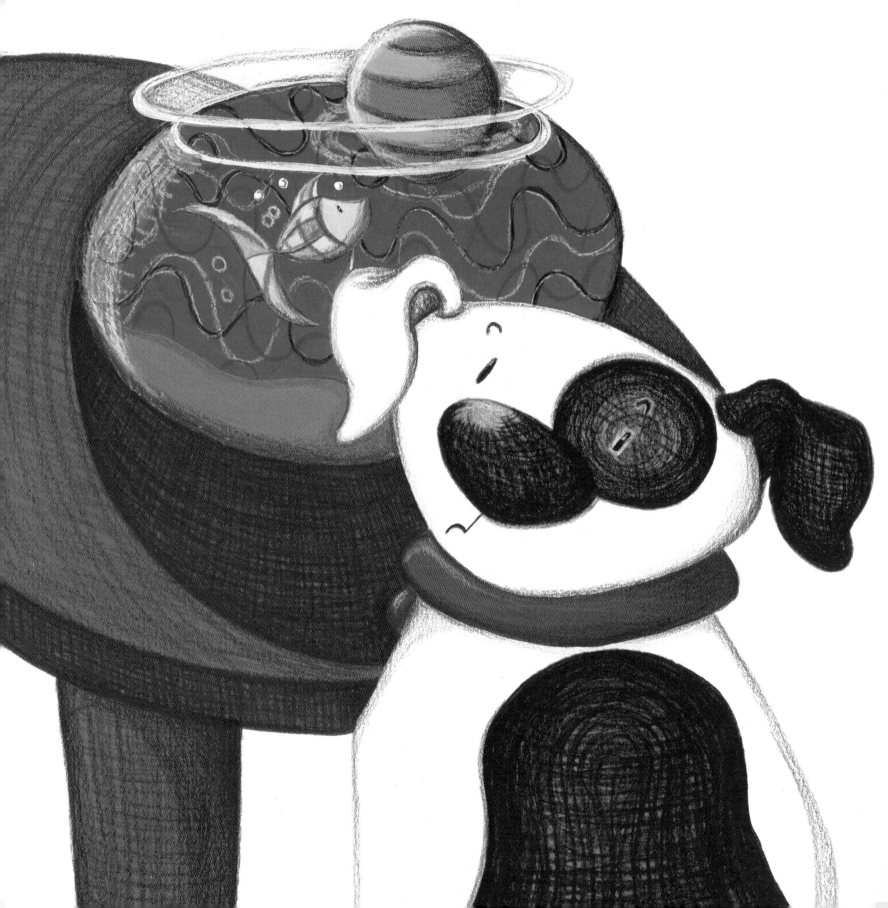

Sam told Bob off for playing ball with Fish.
"Fish don't play ball, Bob," he said.

"Go back to
your basket!"

Sam told him off again when he tried
to share his blanket with Fish...

...and again when he thought
Fish might like a pat on the head.

"Maybe Fish would like to go for a walk," thought Bob.

But when Sam saw Bob drop his leash into Fish's bowl, he got angry.

"Fish don't go for walks, Bob", he said, waggling his finger.

"Go back to your basket!"

Bob loved his basket, but he didn't
like being sent there.
"Fish aren't very exciting,"
thought Bob.
"They don't like any
of the things I like doing."

Bob lay in his basket
and thought very
hard about things.

"Fish don't like blankets,
  or being stroked.

"Fish don't do juggling either.

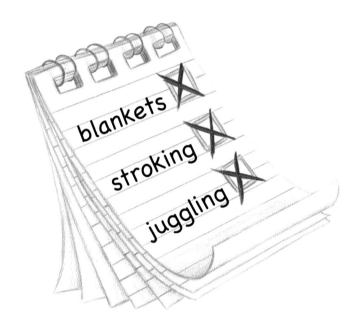

"But worst of all,
        fish don't play ball!"

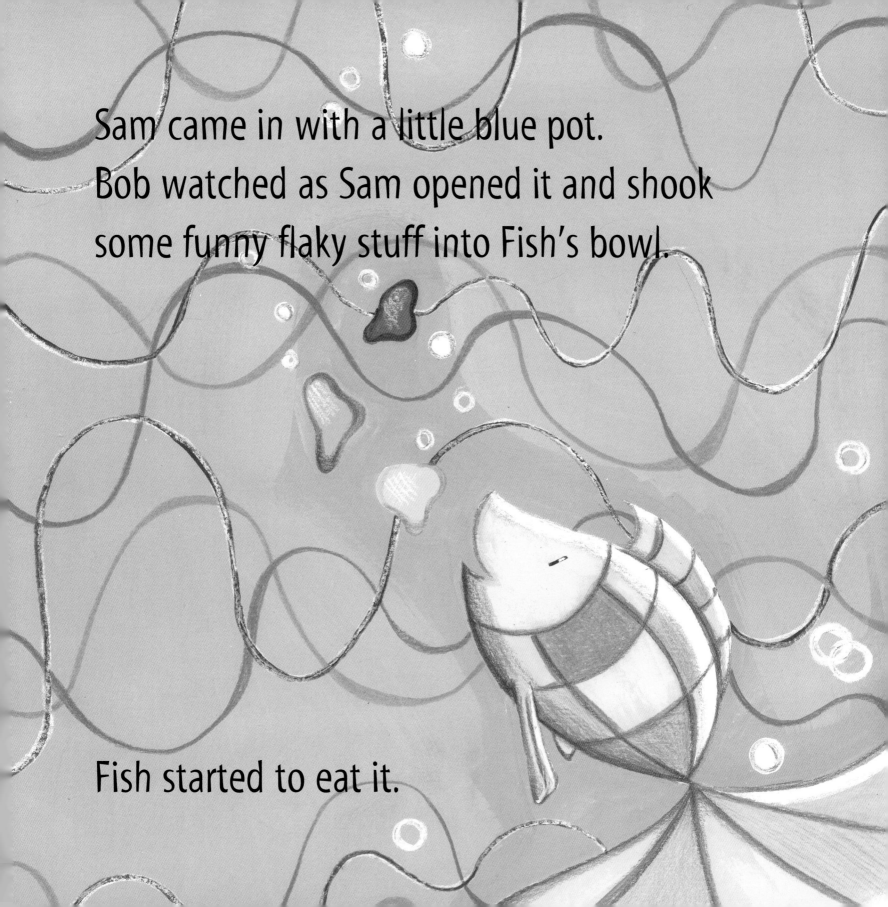

Sam came in with a little blue pot.
Bob watched as Sam opened it and shook
some funny flaky stuff into Fish's bowl.

Fish started to eat it.

"Humpf," thought Bob.
"At least, I suppose, we both like eating."

"Maybe fish aren't so bad after all..."

For Bonnin

With many thanks to Colin and Jake

E.M.

This edition published by Albury Books in 2016
Albury Court, Albury, Thame, OX9 2LP, United Kingdom

Text © Emma McCann • Illustrations © Emma McCann
The rights of Emma McCann to be identified as the author and illustrator have been
asserted by them in accordance with the Copyright, Designs and Patents Act, 1988

ISBN 978-1-910235-09-6 (paperback)

A CIP catalogue record for this book is available from the British Library

Printed in China